D0527384

Text copyright © Rebecca Lisle 2001
Illustrations copyright © David Kearney 2001
Book copyright © Hodder Wayland 2001

Published in Great Britain in 2001
by Hodder Wayland, an imprint of
Hodder Children's Books

The right of Rebecca Lisle to be identified as the
author and David Kearney as the illustrator of this Work
has been asserted by them in accordance with the
Copyright, Designs and Patents Act 1988

British Library Cataloguing in Publication Data

Lisle, Rebecca
  The Bear Pit. – (Tremors)
  1. Horror tales 2. Children's stories
  I. Title
  823.9'14 [J]

ISBN: 0 7502 3685 X

Printed in Hong Kong by Wing King Tong

Hodder Children's Books
A division of Hodder Headline Limited
338 Euston Road, London NW1 3BH

REBECCA LISLE

THE BEAR PIT

Illustrated by David Kearney

HODDER
Wayland

an imprint of Hodder Children's Books

Chapter One

Only Hester knew what had happened to
Jed that night. Nobody else ever found out.
Anyway, nobody would have believed her if
she'd told how Jed *really* got those marks on
his leg…

It was August when cousin Jed arrived from America. He was going to stay with Hester's family while his parents looked for a new house in London.

"Do you think you'll miss living in America?" Hester's mum asked.

"Nah, I think I'll like it here," said Jed. "It's quaint in the countryside. Everything's so small and old."

"Oh, I know, old and *haunted*," laughed Hester's mum. She went into the kitchen to make some tea.

"I'd *love* to see a ghost," said Jed. "Hey!" he added, suddenly. "Hester, have you got an air rifle around here?"

Jed was eyeing up a plump pigeon in the garden.

"What for?" asked Hester suspiciously.

"To shoot that old bird." Jed aimed an imaginary rifle. *"Pop!"*

Hester flushed angrily. "*Shoot it?* You can't! It's… it's *illegal.*"

She didn't know whether it was or not, but she had to stop him somehow. Jed was always showing off and teasing animals. He could be really cruel sometimes.

Jed, shook his head, "Ah, well…" He turned back to Hester. "So, what sort of an address is this Bear Pit Lane, anyway? Have you got bears here or something? We have bears in the States."

Hester sighed. "Well, in Victorian times," she said, "when people were *allowed* to be cruel to animals, there was a bear pit near here. It belonged to a man called George Kyte. He had a house here, too, but it's fallen down now. There's a display at the local museum about him. He kept four big bears down in a pit. They were shackled with chains and metal cuffs around their legs. Mr Kyte made the poor bears dance by poking them and whipping them. People paid to watch them perform."

"Really?" asked Jed, wide-eyed.

"Yes. You can still hear the bears growling in the night and rattling their chains."

"Is that true, Aunt Sylvia?" Jed asked Hester's mum.

"Oh, it is true," said Hester's mum, putting the cups of tea on the table. "The pit is still there, but I don't know about the bears growling and rattling their chains. That's just Hester's imagination."

"Hey, Hester, you've got to take me to see this old bear pit," Jed said.

"No way," said Hester. "I don't like it. No one goes. Everyone's scared of it."

"Oh, please, Hester. I'd really like to see it."

Jed aimed his imaginary rifle through the open window again and made shooting noises. "*I* wouldn't be scared. *I'd* just shoot any old bears I saw," he boasted. "*Pow, pow! Dead!*"

Chapter Two

"*Miaow! Miaow!*"

Hester ran to the window just in time to see Kitty dash across the lawn. A second later Jed appeared from the same direction, laughing.

Hester guessed he'd been taunting the cat. Again. She remembered the pigeon and her blood boiled.

"Hey, Jed!" she called out. "You said you wanted to go to the bear pit. Let's go now, shall we?"

Hester hoped he'd find the place as horrible and upsetting as she did. Maybe then he'd think twice about teasing animals.

Bear Pit Lane was a narrow, dead-end lane with Hester's row of cottages on one side and fields on all other sides.

"This was where Mr Kyte lived," said Hester, pointing to the ruins of a house. "The pit's just over there."

Hester led Jed round behind the ruined house, past tangled thickets of hazel bushes and brambles.

"Here," she said, stopping.

The bear pit was a brick-lined hole, like a wide, deep chimney, set into the side of a slope. At the bottom of the chimney there had been an entrance. Now just a few iron bars hung there like rotten black teeth. In front was a shallow, grassy area where the animals had once performed.

"It's the saddest place, Jed. Can't you feel it? I don't know how anyone could mistreat an animal like that."

Hester stood on the rim of the pit and stared down.

"Isn't it odd how different things grow down there," she said, thoughtfully. "Such dark leaves… Those purple berries look poisonous. Nothing nice or good can grow in such a sad place."

"You and your imagination," mocked Jed. "Girls are peculiar," Jed muttered to himself. "Especially English girls."

The wind freshened and blew Hester's hair round her face. It rippled through the trees with a moaning sound.

"I'm going down there," said Jed.

"No, please don't!"

But Jed had already jumped.

"You idiot!" Hester yelled. "No one goes into the pit."

"Ouch!" Jed was rolling on the ground holding his knee.

"Are you hurt?" asked Hester.

"I must've hit a stone or something," Jed said, without looking at Hester.

He felt dreadful. It was as if he'd jumped into a well of bleakness. Sadness and despair washed over him in cold, sickening waves.

If he met Hester's gaze, she'd see it, too, and she'd know that she'd been right.

Jed didn't want Hester to be right.

"This place isn't haunted," he told himself.

Sweat glistened on Jed's face. His heart thumped. He couldn't swallow. It seemed as if the walls of the pit were closing in around him, cutting out the light and even the air...

"I'm not frightened. I'm not," Jed hissed to himself. "I just hurt my knee."

Taking a deep breath, he began pulling at the weeds, trying to find what had hurt him, trying to push the panic away.

"There's something here!" he shouted. "It's not a stone... It's *metal*."

"Oh, don't," Hester begged him. She knew that it had to be something bad if it was in the bear pit.

Jed forced himself to focus on pulling up his find. His panic began to dissolve.

"Wow! Wait till you see this!" Jed squeezed out from under the broken iron bars, holding the metal object above his head triumphantly. It was easy, now he was out in the open air, to dismiss his fear completely.

"I must have winded myself when I jumped," he thought. "That's all it was."

"Hester, look," he cried. "Look at this!"

It was a rusty metal leg-iron with a chain attached to it. A shackle for a bear.

"Oh, Jed! No! Put it back, please," Hester urged him.

"No way! This must be a hundred years old, maybe more."

Suddenly, Jed spun round. "What was that?" He shivered involuntarily. "Did you hear? It sounded like thunder."

"I didn't hear anything," said Hester. "Please put that back. It's horrible. *Evil.* You *can't* want it."

"Well, I do."

Hester glared at him. "Did I ever tell you that Mr Kyte had a terrible end, Jed? His bears turned on him and ripped him to pieces."

Jed laughed. "So what?" he said. "You can't scare me."

He set off towards the cottage, swinging the leg-iron backwards and forwards on the end of its chain. The squeaking, grinding metal noise was horrible, it even grated on Jed's nerves. The bear pit *had* spooked him for a moment, but he would never tell Hester that.

Chapter Three

Jed sat in the garden cleaning the leg-iron.
Hester watched him.

"It was Mr Kyte's, wasn't it?" he asked,
looking up. "It's great. Bears are so massive,
so strong. Imagine being in total control of
such a powerful animal – fantastic! I'd be
a good animal tamer, I reckon."

"Bears belong in the forest," Hester said angrily. "They need space. They need to be able to go hunting and…"

"Yeah, yeah," said Jed, in a bored voice.

"Oh, what's the point? You'll never understand!" cried Hester.

In the early evening, Jed sat on the porch, holding the leg-iron. He was wondering if everything Hester had told him was true. If people were so scared of the bear pit, and hadn't ever investigated it, maybe there were other things to find.

Jed had to go back. *Alone.* If there was more treasure in the bear pit, he wanted to have it all to himself.

Quietly, he slipped out of the garden. As he made his way to the pit, Jed pictured himself standing there with an admiring audience surrounding him. He'd be wearing fine clothes and brandishing a whip. The bears would be roaring and the audience screaming, but *he* would be in charge.

"I'll show Hester," he thought. "I won't be scared. Last time I'd banged my knee – it was probably just the pain that made me go funny."

Jed was smiling as he descended into the arena. It was very quiet.

Suddenly a blackbird called out in alarm. Its wings beat loudly close to Jed's head, making him jump. A creature scuttled in the grass at his feet.

Jed began to feel uneasy.

In the dusky twilight, Jed could hardly
see. What was that moving? Was that shadow
growing bigger? Coming nearer?

A strong smell wafted through the air,
the smell of wet fur and old meat. *Animal.*

A shiver ran up Jed's spine and tingled
over his scalp. He felt a wild panic rising
inside him. It was worse than the last time.
What was happening?
Then he heard
a low growl.

Jed spun round
and saw the vast
shape of a great
bear coming
towards him. He
nearly screamed,
but was stopped
by the sudden
crack of a whip
slicing the air and
smacking the ground
beside him.

Jed jumped. The silhouette of a tall man wearing a long cloak and top hat loomed out of the shadows. The whip was in his hand.

Mr Kyte.

Crack! the whip lashed out at Jed.

"Owww!" Jed's voice came out like a hurt growl.

Jed tried to move, but he couldn't. His leg was caught in something. He tugged. What was holding it? Then he saw. His leg was circled in a cruel iron ring and chained to a post. And his leg had changed: it was massive and covered in fur.

"*No!*" he cried, but the only sound that came from his mouth was the sad howl of a bear.

"Dance!" roared Mr Kyte, cracking his horrible stinging whip. Jed danced.

Beside him, the other bears bobbed and jigged miserably.

"Up! Up!" shouted Mr Kyte, and Jed pulled his great shaggy body up on to his hind legs, his snout pointing to the sky.

"Bow down!" ordered Mr Kyte and Jed bent his massive body as low as he could, but not before the whip had slashed across his back.

Jed wept, but bears don't cry. He called out for help, but bears can't speak. So he roared and growled and all around him, the other bears did the same.

"Help me," thought Jed. "Stop this nightmare, somebody, please!"

Then, suddenly, Jed heard his name, very faintly, as if someone were calling him from far away. He yanked at his chain and roared, "*Help!*"

"Jed, it's me, Hester."

Hester! The shapes slowly faded and receded into the shadows. The noises died away, the smells disappeared and from across the field came the familiar sound of a wood pigeon's call.

Slowly, Jed went up to Hester. He wondered what she'd seen. He wondered what he would say.

"Are you all right?" she whispered.

Somehow, Jed just couldn't tell Hester the truth. How could he admit to her that he'd been so scared and humiliated?
He opened his mouth… and laughed.

"Ha! I'm fine! This leg-iron must be magic, or something," he said, brightly. "I saw the bears. I was there with Mr Kyte. The bears were dancing and doing tricks, it was fantastic!"

Hester stared at him, and at the tear stains on his face. "Jed, how could you?" she gasped.

"What?"

"I saw you! I saw it all. You're *lying!*"

Chapter Four

"I'm not lying!"

"You are!" Hester shouted. "I saw
everything and it was awful! Keeping that
leg-iron has brought the bears back. You've
got to stop pretending, Jed, this is serious!
What if it happens again?"

Jed shook his head and looked away.

"Look," said Hester, softly, "I brought these tools from Dad's work box. We could destroy the leg-iron. Break it up. If we got rid of it, Jed, maybe the bears would be rid of it, too."

"No. It's mine. I want to keep it. It's magic. Maybe it could transport us back to the past? Imagine what else it can do…"

"How can you say that after what happened? Just think, Jed. The bears might come back. Or you could get stuck being a bear. Jed *listen* to me."

Scowling, Jed shook his head and ran off.

By now the trees were only black shapes against a purple sky as the night darkened around them.

Hester could hardly see as she hurried after Jed. She caught up with him outside the ruins of Mr Kyte's old house. "Wait!" she called. "Please, wait!"

Jed stopped reluctantly and for a moment they stood together, breathing heavily.

A noise startled them.

"What was that?" whispered Hester. "It sounded like… I heard a growl, really I did. Oh, Jed, it's the bears again."

On the path behind Jed and Hester they distinctly heard the pad-pad of heavy paws, the sound of fur swishing softly against fur.

The first cry, a low, throaty rumble, sounded to their right. They spun round, peering into the shadows, but it was too dark to see anything. Immediately it was answered by another, deeper bellow on their left. A sharper, angrier bark echoed from behind them. Then a snarl and growl from in front.

"They're all around us," hissed Hester.
"Jed, this is your fault!"

Jed and Hester stood back to back, staring
into the blackness as the growling grew
closer and closer. Now they could hear the
bears snuffling, grunting and snapping their
teeth. Hester was sure she saw the glint of
their small eyes as they blinked. The air
filled with their bitter smell.

Nearer and nearer they came.

"Surrounded," whispered Hester. "There's only one thing. Quick, give me the leg-iron, Jed! *Now!*"

"No, I want—"

"It's our only chance!"

Hester grabbed it from him, just as damp rough fur brushed against her. She turned and sprinted away.

"Hester! *Help!*" Jed's cry followed her as she ran.

Hester had to destroy the leg-iron before it was too late... She raced up the lane to her cottage and stopped in the light from the porch. Her head was aching and her heart was pounding in her chest like a hammer.

From her bag she took out a heavy spanner and quickly slipped it into the link holding the metal cuff and turned it. The metal was weak and snapped quickly.

Jed limped out of the darkness.

"Jed? Are you OK?"

But Jed didn't reply. He grabbed the spanner and began to smash the leg-iron with it. He beat the leg-iron until the circle of metal had snapped and broken into crumbling, rusty, twisted fragments.

"There… Done." Jed wiped his face wearily. "You were right, Hester. While the leg-iron survived, the pain of the bears survived, too. I wont ever forget their pain, because…" Jed turned and showed Hester his leg. Four parallel streaks of blood patterned it. The marks of the bear.

"Don't tell," whispered Jed. "I don't want anyone to know."

"I promise. Does it hurt a lot?"

"No. Not really. Not compared to how it hurt to be chained up and teased… Only I wouldn't believe it and I'm sorry," added Jed. "The bears showed me what it was like and I ignored them. I was so stupid… But I know now."

"I don't think you'll ever treat animals badly again, will you, Jed?" asked Hester quietly.

Jed shook his head.

Hester never told anyone about that night.

Jed would have liked to forget, but he couldn't. The scratch marks would leave a scar on his leg to remind him.

But only he and Hester ever knew what had caused the scar. They were the only people, in this life, ever to see Mr Kyte and his famous dancing bears.

DARE TO BE SCARED!

Are you brave enough to try more titles in the Tremors series? They're guaranteed to chill your spine...

The Empty Grave by Rebecca Lisle
When Jay visits her cousin at Gulliver House, strange things start to happen. Who is the mysterious child that cries in the night? And what is behind the sealed door? Jay and Freddie must discover the truth before it's too late...

Welcome to the Waxworks by Sam Godwin
Becky has to write a diary of anything interesting that happens during half term. But there's nothing exciting about boring old Skipton. That is, until she visits the waxworks museum and gets more than she bargained for. The exhibits seem so real, so life-like...

Bringing Back the Dead by Belinda Hollyer
When Jamie's dad finds a photograph of their new home, taken in 1879, he has to buy it. But soon Jamie realizes that the figures in the photograph have moved. Then they start to visit Jamie in the night... What do they want? And how can Jamie stop them from haunting him?

All these books and many more can be purchased from your local bookseller. For more information about Tremors, write to: The Sales Department, Hodder Children's Books, A division of Hodder Headline Limited, 338 Euston Road, London NW1 3BH.